HAN M GREENBARG

Byrne

First published by starlighteineadhpress 2022

Copyright © 2022 by Han M Greenbarg

This novel is entirely a work of fiction. The names, characters and incidents portrayed in it are the work of the author's imagination. Any resemblance to actual persons, living or dead, events or localities is entirely coincidental.

First edition

ISBN: 979-8-9866044-0-4

This book was professionally typeset on Reedsy. Find out more at reedsy.com

Better days will come. Be courageous and believe in all that is good. It's going to be okay. Even if it's not. It's going to be okay.

Contents

One

Rosiegirl

⁂

Tuesday June 24th, 2025 12:22 AM

My stories help her live. That's what she tells me. I like speaking to her in the voices of my fictional characters...using my own voice when I deem it necessary. Pretending to be someone else makes me feel safe. The pain and the fear is not as bad when I hide in the worlds I create. A shield from this living nightmare. We are together in this and it's not ending. I can't see it getting better.

We are all scared. We are all trapped.

The blue light is dying. A low buzzing tone in the corridors. All the doors closed and locked. We are waiting for the final call of the night. Waiting for the scream of the beaten. Someone always gets beaten. Someone always makes them angry.

Been five months since the lockdown of our city. The world is contaminated by the Omnadie plague and we exist by the rule of the cruel Oficialkers. Every corner of our building lives under camera eyes and no resident is exempt from the authoritarian treatment. The middle night hours are the most terrifying.

"Rosiegirl, you awake?"

"Yeah."

"Care to hear a new character idea?"

She yawns. I can hear her mumbling something. We talk to each other in the night, sitting with our backs to the thin wall that divides us. I think she gets tired of my story ideas. Maybe not all of them. Been awhile of us learning about each other and I still don't know if she truly thinks I'm likable or not. Maybe I'm too weird.

Imagination is survival.

I'll do almost anything to not see another suicide. But I don't really blame the Sick and Tired troupe. When you've had enough you've had enough, right? I blame the Oficialkers. They love beating us up when we break a rule. There are too many rules to remember and when humans are hungry, thirsty, tired, delusional…they act crazy. You can't expect crazy people to follow your strict rules. You can't expect crazy people to stay in line. Clashes are inevitable.

"What's the new character, Byrne?"

"I'm not Byrne. I'm Jak."

"Okay." She yawns again. "Tell me the character."

"Okay," I say with a grin. I put my hands up in front of me as I lay out the scene. "First comes a pack of unicorns ridden by agitated Elves from a country devoid of magic. The leader of the pack is the most trouble making of the Elves. His name is Faunderick."

"Faunderick? That's weak material for you, Byrne."

"No. Not Byrne," I say in a crooning Scottish accent. "Jak MacEaldan."

2

"How about Thuraudane? That's robust. Elves need sexy, robust names."

I can tell that she is smiling. I know about her love of Elves because I encourage it. "All right. You've bested me, little warrior," I say.

"Yes," she says proudly. "What's the name of the country?"

"Winewater. Simple and evocative."

"I thought you liked to be more goofy. That doesn't sound like you."

"No?"

"No. How about we give this a rewrite tomorrow?"

My back is sticky with sweat. The horrible summer makes the lockdown so much worse. None of us have balconies. No breeze from the windows and they refuse to fix the air conditioning. I slide to the floor, taking my glasses off and wiping sweat from my nose. The same beads of sweat sting my eyes. Torture. Heat is torture.

"Rewrite. Okay, Rosiegirl. I'll rewrite what you think I should."

"Oh, Byrne," she says in a sultry whisper, "I have a surprise for you. At sunrise."

"Runsire," I say. We share a chuckle. *Runsire.* Our favorite made-up word.

"Yeah. Runsire. Night, Byrne."

6:49 AM

I knock on her door dressed in a baggy suit and tie. Today I'm my high class character Ronny Winters. Sometimes I don't need to use an accent or change my vocal tone…often a costume is enough to help me face the real world and the real people in it.

"Hey, Byrne," she says as she opens the door.

3

"Whoa," I say. This must be the surprise.

"What?"

"You chopped your hair."

"Yeah."

"Now you look even more like a bombshell agent Elf warrior." I so badly want to lean in to kiss her mouth and plant my nose on her neck where she spritzes the best smelling cedar-orange perfume.

"It matches Rosiegirl?"

"It does. You look perfect."

I know some residents will take one look at her and scoff or wonder why in the wonderful universe she cut her lovely apple red hair, but my heart won't stop racing when I see her. So fierce and messy...the spitfire of my world.

"Wanna have breakfast?" She waves a hand behind her. "I microwaved oatmeal."

Her apartment is just as disastrous as mine. Piles of clothes scattered across the floor like molehills, books sliding out of their home shelves, plastic plates and utensils overflowing in the trash can.

"Sure. I never turn down oatmeal. Brown sugar?"

"Apple cinnamon," she says. "You cleaned me out of the brown sugar a week ago, remember?"

"Sorry."

"You apologize too much."

"Sorry again."

"It's fine, Byrne."

I can't believe that she even lets me into her apartment now. Our first encounter was in front of the building. I was going to take a walk in the city just as she was dragging a big box of her stuff toward the ground floor door.

One Month Before The Lockdown

I feel like I'm in a movie scene as I watch her struggle to pick up the box. This feels like the start of a romantic comedy or maybe even a poorly written thriller...

"Hey, do you need help with that?"

"No. I got it."

"I don't mind helping you."

"No thank you."

She reminds me of the women I've met who get offended when a man tries to be the hero in a bad situation. She must be relentlessly stubborn like that too, so I say, "You're one of those, huh?"

"Yeah, one of those," she says, apparently reading my mind.

I realize I should just walk away instead of watching her fumble with the box, but the way she's working to figure out the best way to pick it up without spilling her stuff is very entertaining. She's cute.

"Darn it!" she yells as several books slide out.

I'm wondering why she tried so hard to fit everything in to the point where it's a literal mountain. She growls and bends down to pick them up. It's now a cascade of stuff on the sidewalk.

"Here." I bend down with her, grabbing one of the hardcover books. I see that it's one of mine. The third book in my Warrior Run series. My trying-to-be-cool face is on the back cover. "You like fantasy thrillers?"

"What?"

"Fantasy thrillers. Like this one?" I ask.

"Yeah," she says without looking at me.

I gently lay the book down and continue helping her put stuff back into the box. It's at a tipping point again, but now that I've formed the Mountain Of Things, I don't want to see another avalanche.

"Thank you," she says, and rapidly begins to tell me why she came here. "My boyfriend works a few hours from here. I came to get things ready for when he comes back to surprise me with a proposal."

"You know he's going to propose?"

"I'm eighty percent sure of it. He drops hints all the time on video chat. I want to be set in my own career before we get married. I'll be thriving in business in six months."

"You're building a career in less than a year?"

"Well, I don't know. He let me choose our relocation place because I found a group of independent stores who want to sell my ear cuffs and stackable rings."

"Fascinating. I've always been curious of independent jewelers. Can I use that in my next book?"

She snaps her head up, finally giving me a chance to see her eyes. "Uh…I guess."

I smile.

"Wait. Oh my gosh." She picks up the book I had just held. "You're this guy. Maddox Byrne."

I'm finding it funny that we are both kneeling down across from each other on a public sidewalk with a Mountain Of Things in the middle. All I can do is keep smiling and hope I don't bust into a laugh. "That's me," I say. "Nice to meet you."

Her eyes are sparkling in the sunlight. She looks like a warrior princess who just found a magical amulet. "Lizzie McCabe," she says, talking extra loud in her excitement. "Why are you living here, Mr. Byrne? This isn't the fanciest apartment building."

"What do you mean?"

"Aren't you like millions of dollars into success? You have like over a dozen books published, right?"

"Lizzie, even if I had ten million in my bank account, I'd choose to live here over anywhere."

"Why?"

I gesture to the sidewalk and street in front of us. "The people. The city. It's full of character."

"Oh." She chuckles. "Yeah, it sure is."

I move to sit directly on the concrete and Lizzie mirrors me. She's blushing as she looks toward a violinist and guitarist rocking out on a street corner.

"You know who you look like?" I say.

"Who?"

"The heroine in Warrior Run. Rosiegirl."

"Oh yeah?"

"Yeah. Page sixteen reads: 'And every move she made was elegant, purposeful, even the fringe of her cloak touching the marble floor with honorable abandon. Never would a man dare to cross her virtue of silver. Rosiegirl astounded without force and without word. Yet she ran wild when beyond the wall...'"

Lizzie looks at me, listening intently to every word.

"'...and her eyes burned dignity and white flame. She was everything they needed to survive the fortnight of battle. Everything a real warrior was and should be.'" I end the passage with a slow breath.

She's quiet, seeming faraway in her own head. Then she says, "You haven't stalked me, have you?"

"No. I would never do that. Just a coincidence." *Not a coincidence, Byrne.* "Would it bother you if I called you Rosiegirl?"

She gets up, returning to her battle with the box. "You can call me that. I really like the character."

"Thank you. Are you sure I can't help you carry that?"

7

"I'm sure. So, if Rosiegirl wasn't inspired by me, where did you get the idea for her?"

"I was driving to a book signing and stopped for ice cream at this family run place. The lady who gave me the ice cream looked like an elvish warrior princess."

Just when I think we had crafted a strong rapport, Lizzie aka Rosiegirl makes that scrunched up weirded out facial expression that ninety nine percent of other people make when I tell them my idea origins. "Okay...that's different," she says.

I feel like an idiot. "Yeah." I know I'm not really an idiot, but each time a pretty girl gives me that look it's such a bummer.

"Okay. Yes. Finally getting this." Rosiegirl grunts as she pushes the box along the ground toward the door. She's got a strong core and legs.

"Hey, it's a good thing I'm not wearing my trench coat, hm? I'd look a little shady then." *Don't know why I just said that. Why did that come out of my mouth? I'm running out of relevant topics.*

"Yes. You would look shady."

I hold the door open for her to push the box through it. "Rieleana wears one in my series."

"I remember. The second book. She's the daughter of Watermatch."

"Wow," I say. Her knowledge of my story makes me smile.

"You choose such strange names for your characters." She breathes out hard on her last push of the box, eyes on the elevator.

"Not good?"

"No, I love it. More unique. Stands out on the shelf."

"Thanks. That's what I always go for."

She grins at me. "Well, I appreciate you holding the door open."

"Welcome. But I think you're going to burn yourself out trying to push that up all the stairs. What floor you on?"

"There's an elevator, Mr. Byrne."

"Yeah, but…"

She realizes and groans. "Oh no."

I point to the stairs. "Yeah. Elevator hasn't worked since I came here."

"They don't fix it?"

"They don't."

Rosiegirl shakes her head, then starts pushing the box to the stairs. "Mr. Byrne, I hate asking, but if I try to carry this stuff by myself I'm never getting to the tenth floor."

I lift one end of the box as she takes the other. "My pleasure, Rosiegirl. I'm on the tenth floor too."

She watches me carefully step backward up the stairs. "You really don't have to though."

"I want to. And you can call me Maddox."

"Byrne," she says with a smile. "I like your last name. It's really cool."

Byrne. Byrne and Rosiegirl. We swap stories all the way up the stairs, talking about random animal encounters in the city and the wild dialogues between drunk and raging people. We learn that we both like our alone time and that we prefer silence over rowdy places. We're both artists…words and jewelry. And I make a friend. A really beautiful friend.

Two

Tower 881

Wednesday June 25th, 2025 3:18 PM

We all gave nicknames to each other on the third day of the lockdown. You might call it a collaborative quirk. Something playful and funny to ease our fears.

"Hey, Storyteller."

"Hey, Wildride."

My three o'clock walk down the corridor is met with scattered high fives and stir-crazy kids peeking out their apartment doors. According to the Oficialkers, anyone could be tainted with plague. Sick or not, we are punished for it. Treated like spies and murderers in our own country. That's how I feel at least.

"Got chosen for the outside today?"

"Yeah. I'll see ya at four."

Wildride is a frenemy living six doors down from me. He has the most epic dreadlocks and is always practicing some kind of funky dance move...he's a former hip hop dance instructor. I like to get into impromptu dance contests with him. My go-to dance is the shuffle. I can do a few decent variations of it and it's probably the only cool thing about me.

I walk down the flights of stairs and start looking for my sneakers in the communal shoe rack. No one wears shoes inside the building. We have to put on our shoes at the rack to go out and take them off when coming in.

"924, your hour is not yet. Go back."

"I'm just waiting."

"Go back."

"I can stand here if I want to."

The armored guard moves away, eyes and metal stick coiled for attack. Without saying anything else, I pick out my shoes and sit down against the wall. I like to watch the door before I go outside. I can't see much past the barred glass, but it's the amazing sunlight I don't get upstairs. The sun. Humans need to feel the sun.

At the risk of the guard beating me for lingering with nothing to do in his presence, I take out my little college-ruled notebook and start scribbling a new story idea. Fear awakens the mind… the subconscious thirsts for excitement…*A six month journey? Ten months? No.* I scratch it out. *Main character…tall, goatee, hay yellow hair, obsessed with jumping off of towers.*

"Hey, Story!"

Castles made of ice and pathways of blue stone. Sapphire? A king and queen walk it. Their soldiers…

"Story!"

I feel someone tapping my shoulder. I look back. Confused. *Kings and queens of ice and rock.*

"You okay?"

"Yeah, I'm…" I shake my head. "Sorry, Wild, I was….."

11

"Fantasy world, huh?"

"How long you been calling my name?" *Light streams through the windows. Placid, ethereal colors.*

Wildride glances at his watch while chewing gummy worms. "About ten minutes."

One of the rough things about being a writer is that when I space out into my story world or act out a scene all by myself, I have people thinking I've gotten high or gone psychotic. More often than not I'm lost in my own imagination and it's the happiest place that I know.

"There's a unicorn standing to the right of you," I say.

"Yeah sure."

Kings and queens of ice and rock. The queen looks like a feisty warrior instead of a royal. Hmm. What does her king think of that? He must like it. What are their names? I think it through, forcing myself to engage in a real conversation. "You don't care about getting hassled by the guard either?"

"Nah. The worst he can do is beat me to the ground. Maybe arrest me. But I'll still be breathing."

"Yeah," I say. "Don't let the mean overlord steal your thunder."

We both look over at the guard now standing with his face to the wall. He hears everything but tries not to listen. Or maybe he tries to listen but can't stand hearing us.

"You don't usually come down before the hour starts, do you, Wild?"

"I don't. But I see you doin it. Thought if we swap dance moves we make a good team. Ya know. Waitin for the tiny bit of freedom."

"Pacing behind a barred and barbed gate is not real freedom to me."

"Feeling the sun is. If I'm gonna be sticky and humid in here,

I better taste the natural cause of the discomfort out there."

"Very poetic, Wild."

He's six-four and I'm five-seven so we definitely look like a weird pair hanging out in the lobby.

"Have you ever explored the other floors?"

"I've been up to the twentieth," he says.

"Not to the top? The thirtieth?"

"Don't have reason to."

"Not even the roof? I love it up there. I can feel the real air even better with that kind of view."

Wildride offers me one of his gummy worms. "What if you get locked out?"

"Never happened," I say, taking the candy.

"Well, what if it did?"

Sigh. Another wasteful debate is coming. I just think he gets tired of talking to his brothers on video chat. He wishes they could visit in person.

"Check it, Story. Almost four." He looks down at his watch. "Ready? And..."

The Horn Of Aermad. We both swivel our heads toward the sound. It goes off at each new hour. As a mom, dad, and their son are told to come back in, Wildride and I prepare to go out. I reach down to give the little boy a high-five as he comes through the door. "Hi, Earthquake."

"Hi, Story. I saw the birds outside. Mommy showed me how to talk to them. You whistle like this!"

"Sweet sound, Earth," I say at his spitting and whistling combo. I lower my voice to add, "But the guard might not like you spitting on the floor."

"I'm not spitting," Earthquake loudly whispers. "It's bird-talking."

13

"924, go out!" the guard shouts at me. He lunges forward and I motion for the little guy and his parents to hurry back to their apartment.

"Mr. Overlord," I grumble under my breath, joining Wildride outside in the cramped space between Tower 881's front door and the First Checkpoint.

We are allowed to go out on a rotational basis in groups of three or four. There is no view except for a twelve foot barred gate and the guards in black and grey suits. To reach the Second Checkpoint and walk on the public street means having to battle it out through a ferocious game of Old Maid or Go Fish.

"So, Story, what's the deal with you and Rosiegirl?"

I see Wildride lighting a cigarette and shuffle three steps to the right...not that it'll keep me away from the smoke. "What deal?"

"Why haven't you told her you love her?"

"I can't tell her that."

"Everybody knows." He tosses me the half-eaten bag of gummy worms.

"She might not feel the same."

"Why don't you just kiss her already? She looks like she wants a kiss."

He's smiling in a way that I don't like. Must be thinking about Rosiegirl as if she was his...

"That's a scoundrel's move," I say. "I can't just do that."

"You're always talking in your weird character voices."

"So what? I'm a writer."

"But I think she likes the real Maddox Byrne. I think she'd like if the real Byrne swept her into his arms and made out with her like it's the end of the world. I mean, c'mon, man, who wouldn't wanna kiss her? She's super sexy."

I'm stunned. Despite me wanting to punch him for fantasizing about her, his scenario about Rosiegirl sounds epic.

"Besides," he says, "the world's ending anyway."

"What?"

"Don't you think?"

"Umm…" I don't like thinking about an end to anything. Suppose it is ending. *If that's true…well…maybe Rosiegirl and I should…*

"I'm gonna get a beer."

"But the hour's hardly started, Wild."

He shakes his head as he shoulders past me to the door. "You can enjoy it for the both of us."

Few people seem to tolerate my company for more than a few minutes. I've gotten used to it. I'm sure that he just called me a weirdo in his mind.

"Alone yet not alone," I say to the sky.

It stings a bit to watch people smirk as they walk away, but the strangeness is still a gift. Everywhere I go I have a group of characters chatting in my head. So even if I feel or look alone…I never am. Pretty cool really. Rosiegirl thinks it is anyway. At least…I hope she does. My imaginary worlds are everything to me.

Three

Cream Cheese On Graham Crackers

Imagination Is Survival

Three weeks into the lockdown I found Rosiegirl sobbing in the corridor, one hand tugging her hair over her face, the other clutching her phone as if it was a childhood teddy bear.

Her boyfriend had killed himself.

She stayed in her apartment for two days, and I made sure not to do any character voices or act out any scenes near our shared wall. But eventually Rosiegirl came back out into the corridor. Tired eyes. Disheveled hair.

"Hi," I said.

"Hey, Byrne."

That's when I offered a hug…which most people will never do because of how paranoid they are of catching Omnadie. But she hugged me back. Ten seconds into the embrace and a random question popped into my head. "Do you want to eat my favorite food?"

"What is it?"

Doubted she would like it, but I told her anyway. "Cream cheese on graham crackers."

She looked up. "That sounds transformative, Byrne."

"Is that a yes?"

She went from just looking at me to giggling. It was the sort of loopy, delusional giggle that people do when trying to fight back tears.

And today we're eating cream cheese on graham crackers while discussing random scenarios in my apartment. She's crazy for cream cheese now. Too bad it's becoming harder to order through grocery delivery.

Thursday June 26th, 4:05 PM

"What are you planning for the next therapy session?"

"Well, I was hoping you would bring the snacks again."

"Sure, Byrne. I can do that." She smiles as she spreads strawberry cream cheese on her floofwich.

"Your eating habits are fascinating, fluttering dove," I say in my Jak MacEaldan voice.

"Thanks. I'm so glad we haven't had a shortage of marshmallow fluff yet."

I don't know why, but watching her create her own quirky food combinations is the cutest thing in the world. I mean… aside from everything else that she does.

Rosiegirl taught me about making a proper floofwich on the second day we were neighbors. In her definition, a floofwich is a marshmallow spread and a single cinnamon graham cracker between two plain pieces of bread. The top bread piece must be white bread, and the bottom piece must be whole grain. Only now she has added my cream cheese to the mix.

"I think one of the kids should lead the session this time. I

17

know Dingo would love to do it."

"Yeah." She works on organizing beads and cords by color while taking bites of the floofwich. She brings her craft tray whenever she comes over just to have a place for her jewelry making.

"When are you gonna do more of those metal ear cuffs? They're pretty."

"I don't know. I'm on a roll with these bracelets." She has her head down, messy red hair in her eyes. Her shirt is super cute today. It's a cartoon picture of two coffee mugs with some random pun between them. She loves word humor just as much as I do.

"When are you coming up to the roof with me? It's really nice."

"I don't like it," she says. "I've seen too many jumpers. Reminds me of…"

Oh. Right. The boyfriend. "Sorry."

She looks up at me as she shifts from a cross-legged position to being on her knees. Her shorts are dark blue. Looks so good with her red hair and off-the-shoulder shirt. "Don't be sorry, Byrne. I know you love the roof."

"Yeah. It's fun playing games with the kids up there."

"I'm glad you have fun with them."

I focus in on her fingers, the way she's braiding dark red cords into a bracelet. She's shifting into super concentration mode.

"Hey, uh, Rosie, I gotta go see Alchemist and Everwhen." I get up, not really wanting to walk away from this cute scene in my apartment. "You can hang out here as long as you want to."

"Oh yeah," she says. "It's almost five. You gonna have dinner with them?"

"I don't know. Rather cook something with you."

"It's okay." She smiles at me as I head for the door. "Say hi for me, Byrne."

"I will. Everwhen usually asks about you."

On Thursdays I have microwave popcorn and citrus tea with Alchemist and his wife Everwhen. They're always in a robe and slippers and their tiny television has the food channels on it. They claim to like my company because they were ghostwriters before retiring and they understand how my mind works. I doubt that though. The only thing we really bond over is cheering for the pre-selected contestants on the cooking shows.

5:15 PM

"Hi, Storyteller."

"Hey, Everwhen. How's your day been?"

"Just knitting."

"Oh." I look at the scarf dangling inches from the floor, wondering why she's making such a thing in the middle of summer. "That's pretty."

"Thank you. Want some popcorn?"

"Yeah, sure." I join Alchemist in front of the television, sitting myself in the second recliner. *How is it that so many people have recliners in this building?*

"What's up, Storyteller? Any new writing?"

"Nah."

He passes the popcorn bowl to me. "Bet the guy from Boston's gonna win the cake decorating challenge."

I look at the screen. *Hmm. Well, maybe.* "I don't know, Alchemist. Those women look ready to throw down some heat."

"Yeah right."

"H0n?" Everwhen calls from her corner. I can't tell if she's talking to me or her husband.

19

"Yeah?" Me and Alchemist say together. He looks at me with a half-smile, laughs, and uproariously coughs into his mug of lukewarm tea.

"Story," Everwhen says. "I meant you. Want some tea with your popcorn?"

I'm still looking back at Alchemist, both of us in silent agreement that what we just did was silly. But his wife does call a lot of people 'hon'. Easy to get mixed up, isn't it? Anyone could be a hon to her.

"Yeah, Everwhen. I'll take some tea. I can heat it myself."

"No, no." She wildly waves her hand at me when I stand up. "Sit. I'll bring it to you, Story."

"Thanks." I almost never drink tea in any other circumstance. But this couple got me into a routine with them and now tea is just part of it. Tea and popcorn. The citrus flavor doesn't clash too bad with the buttery popcorn...well, it'd be nicer if Alchemist knew how to pop it right. Burnt pieces always overwhelm the bowl.

"Writing any other fantasy books?" Everwhen asks.

"No," I say. "I think Warrior Run took it out of me."

"Oh, I bet you'll write more fantasy, hon."

"Maybe."

"Look!" Alchemist bumps me with his elbow. "Story, I told you that he'd do it!"

"Do what?" I toss a terribly charred popcorn piece into my mouth. Tastes like coal. "The competition hardly started."

"Fine, but he did it already in his mind. I know it! Boston guys always get the prize."

I grin at Alchemist's enthusiasm for a show he's seen a million times. *Is this what happens when we age? We take more pleasure in reruns instead of current episodes?* It's the same thing whenever I come to visit them. Same shows, same chairs, same popcorn, and same citrus tea that Everwhen says she'll bring to me but takes at least twenty minutes to actually do it because she's laser-focused on a knitting mission.

My life. One hour of it at least. What in the world am I doing?

Four

Dingo

Friday June 27th, 2025 1:21 PM

If I have to start running for any reason there is one scenario that plays in my mind. It's always me leading old world soldiers across a blood-soaked battlefield. I wear a white and silver uniform and carry a sword and shield. I hear music in my head as I run. Something with really fast, dramatic violins and maybe a little piano and drums too.

Half the residents call my imaginative scenarios fever dreams. But they aren't. I'm wide awake when I imagine all of it. My writer mind may have some disturbing elements to it, but I promise it's no dream. It's my pretend reality.

"No time to talk, Garage! Trolls are chasing me!"

"What?"

I answer without looking back. "I stole their amulet!"

Today is one of those days...those days where I race as fast as I can up all the flights of stairs leading to the roof. Usually it's just a really long walk. But today I run.

"You're such an idiot!" Garage yells.

"Thanks, I forgive you!" I say and keep running.

If I had time to engage every insult it'd be at least a year's worth of sitting in a circle passing out verbal forgiveness.

"Boo!" Six-year-old Dingo jumps in front of me and laughs when he sees my startled face. I'm pretending to be scared this time...he always jumps out like this.

"What are you doing on this floor, buddy?" I ask.

"I'm playing with my friend."

I look back at the open door and see his little girl friend Ladybug peeking around the corner. I smile and wave to her.

"Wanna play tag with us, Storyteller?" Dingo asks.

"I can't. I'm running from the trolls."

His eyes grow big. "Trolls are here?"

"Yeah," I whisper.

Dingo nervously looks around before tugging at my arm. I drop to a knee. "What, buddy?"

"Can I run with you?"

I grin and turn around, offering him a ride on my back. "Jump up."

"Yay!"

"We have to hurry!" I say.

"Run fast, Story!"

I never understood people who didn't see pirates in line at a buffet or silver-maned dragons leading therapy sessions. Every scenario in my imagination is alive and special to me. But no one I know can see it like I do. It's made for a pretty rough growing up.

The first time I talked out loud about my story characters was when I was three years old. My mom and dad said they would find me out of bed and munching peanut butter cereal while watching some scary movie I was too young for. I managed to sneak out of my room a lot, and each time I did it, I was in the middle of talking to my characters.

To a person who doesn't have my mind, I look and sound like I'm mentally insane. But I promise I've never been insane. I'm a writer.

Tenor the Food Bringer greets us from behind, and Dingo yells, "Oh no! It's the volcano lion!"

I laugh as I turn my head. "The what?"

"Hurry, Story! He's helping the trolls get us!"

We take a detour on the twenty-third floor to greet a young-at-heart mom and her two teenage girls who love playing their pretend rock band since they can't afford instruments. They let me jump in with my air keyboard from time to time when I walk past their door. The girls might think I'm cute but I've never been sure. I appreciate that they don't insult me as women sometimes do for being my strange self.

I often like to add a flair by spinning around as I play my invisible keys and head bang to their air guitar and drums.

"You came in late!" Adorbs tells me.

"Hard to know," I say with a grin.

"Mom says you're a dork," Silvercrown says. She shakes her pink bangs out of her eyes as she goes into a drum solo.

"But it's good," Adorbs says. "Dorky is better than creepy."

With Dingo still riding on my back, I don't have the energy or maneuverability to do my usual air keyboard, but I say hi to them through the open door before Dingo yells in my ear that we have to keep running from the volcano lion.

"I'm going! He's not gonna get us!"

"He will! We have to be on the roof, Story!"

The roof. The roof is safe.

When I want to release tension or anguish I howl like a wolf on the roof. A primal mourning sound to honor the pain of others and myself. It feels good to go rogue like that. Dingo and I howl and yip to let the mountain Elves know that we made it alive, and then I reveal the lemon lollipops I'd saved and give one to him.

He smiles at me, unwraps it, and sits down with the cityscape view. I sit with him. "Hey buddy, what was that thing about the volcano lion?"

"I made it up. It's a lion who lives in lava."

"What does it look like?"

"I think he's mostly red. Some spiky fireballs in his hair."

"I'm gonna use that in my next book."

"Really?"

"May I?"

"Yes. Can I name him?"

"Okay. Tell me the name."

Dingo stands up quickly, waving his lollipop around as he acts out a brand new scene with the volcano lion. "Wildfire! Wildfire is scary! He bites with lava!"

"Oh my goodness," I say with wide eyes. I watch him hop around acting like a hyper animal. The roof is hot on bare feet, but luckily we're safe in a small spot of shade. "Does he howl?"

"No! Volcano lions don't howl, Story! He roars."

"How about I howl as a wolf and you roar as a lion?"

"But I like howling more."

I laugh at his pout and reach over to catch the lollipop before it falls from his hand. "Okay. We can both howl again."

I only sacrifice a little of my waning energy to let out wolf yips and howls with Dingo before he sits next to me, crossing his legs like mine and asking for the lollipop back.

"Story, why don't more people come up here?"

We can smell the urban fumes of the city from the roof...not pleasant. Not comforting. We can hear aggressive shouts of the Oficialkers, honking of the service vehicles, but no happy music from street performers or cheering of park concertgoers. Life in this place is not built for thriving.

"They're scared," I tell him. "They're scared to come up here."

"Why?"

"It's a good thing you don't know." *Just keep being a kid, little guy. Just keep being a kid. Don't grow up yet.*

I worry about him seeing jumpers falling from other buildings. I try my best to keep the kids safe from the increasing terror, but not all of them look away in time. And some were torn from their parents when their parents tested positive for the plague. The new system doesn't protect the kids. They don't care about the babies and toddlers crying. Humanity is not breaking because of the plague...it's the bad people who destroy them.

"C'mon, Dingo. Let's get you home."

2:50 PM

Dingo and his uncle live in the apartment across from mine.

"Hi, Mr. Pardon. Brought your nephew back safe."

Pardon gulps beer in his recliner and belches. "Safe from what?"

"From trolls, Uncle," Dingo says with a grin.

Pardon isn't a smiley or chatty guy, but as far as I know he treats his nephew well. I glance at the television to see what he's watching. Another old baseball game. "Did you try that eagle scene yet?"

"Naw. It's stupid," he says, sinking lower into the chair.

"It'll make you feel happy," I say.

"Pretending to fly is stupid."

"I'm sure you'll get into it eventually." I look to Dingo who is watching me from his mattress on the kitchen floor and we trade silent salutes before I leave. He's lost in his coloring book.

3:15 PM

"Food Bringer came by when you were out. I put your groceries next to mine." Rosiegirl points to the counter as I come in through her door.

"Yeah. I was on the roof with Dingo."

"Howling like wolves again?"

"Yeah. Well, we howled and then growled because the little guy likes lions."

"Food Bringer said Dingo called him a volcano lion."

I chuckle, loving how Rosiegirl doesn't even question the dialogue. She's used to me and Dingo's ridiculous adventures. "He did. We were running from trolls. He saw Wildfire and had to warn me."

"Wildfire." She stands on her toes to put a box of cinnamon cereal in the cabinet above the sink. "Is that the name of the volcano lion?"

"You get us so well," I say.

"Dingo is your mini-me. You two were made to be buddies."

"Yeah. Sometimes I wonder why I gave up on getting married and having a kid of my own."

Rosiegirl holds out a bag of pretzels and I take it. "You'd be a good dad."

"Thanks."

"It's really sweet how you get along with the kids so well."

"I just want them to feel happy." I lean back into a chair, crunching a pretzel. "No fear."

"I know. It's hard not to worry about the stuff going on outside."

"Least you have your jewelry to distract you, huh?"

"Yeah." She smiles. "It helps. And my book collection helps too. Haven't read any in awhile though."

I glance at the stack of books behind me. Rosiegirl must be reorganizing them…or just making a bigger mess like I do. *Messy people unite.* I'm happy to see the Warrior Run books right on top. "Did you always love books?" I ask. "Or was it a special piece of literature that captured your mind?" *Maybe my books were the catalyst. Catalyst. Hmm. What a great word.*

"My parents read to me and my sisters every night even after we turned into moody teenagers. Then I found my own books and read to myself."

"Bet you were adorable when you were little."

She shrugs. "I guess."

Rosiegirl's so easy to talk to. Even if I'm too nervous about professing my love, I can still discuss every day memories and ideas with her. "When I was two years old my parents would take me to the local used bookstore and I toddled around the bookshelves, pulling the most bizarre titles out. I would cradle each book and my mom said I refused to let her carry it to the register."

"Let me guess, Byrne. You started writing stories at three."

"No. Took a bit longer. But I was spouting stories ever since I could talk. Drove everyone crazy during the big holiday gatherings."

"Someone has to keep things interesting in this lockdown," she says. "I'm glad it's you."

"Me too." I watch her turn to rinse a gathering of mugs, thinking how great it would be if she let me come and wrap my arms around her, holding her against me. Stroking her hair, slow dancing barefoot on the tile, soft kisses on her lips.

"So, you got anything else planned today?"

"No," I say. "Just more daydreaming."

"Sounds fun. I'm gonna work on my leather bracelets today."

I love when she works with leather. Makes me think of a medieval artisan. She's a wonder with various fabrics, shiny accents, and etching kits. Sort of like a shopkeeper in one of those online games who has everything a traveler could want... *except instead of forcing you to wait until you have enough coinage to buy it she just makes it and gifts it to you on the spot.*

"Byrne, what are you thinking about?"

"Oh. Just...you know...shopkeepers in online fantasy games."

Her face is both confused and amused. "Oh. Yeah, I know about those. They tempt you with all their stock but you have to wait to get more gold to trade with them."

Wow. Girl gets me. "Yeah. Right."

"That's really random," she says.

Normal for me.

"But it's definitely an average tangent for a writer like you."

"Yeah." I groan internally. *Embarrassing. Just one of those things. Writer mind things. You're good, Byrne. You're not crazy. She doesn't think you're crazy.*

Five

Teacher

7:32 PM

My editors always complained about me because I had a habit of bending the rules they gave. I turned their staunch directions into wayward suggestions and I often published my books in a style and format that the elite people scoffed at. But the everyday people loved my weird style of words and spacing. They craved originality. They craved story. They still do.

I've spent the past four years teaching a creative writing class at a community college...my techniques are seen as unconventional to say the least, but there were always students on the waiting list. I think they liked how I did my thing and never apologized for it.

The class is still going on through the magic of internet video chat. Blackouts are rapidly happening in different parts of the city, so I only see two students online in this week's class.

"I have one assignment today in regards to writing your

memoir."

"Which is?"

I turn the sound up before answering Caden, noticing that he and Lasee are intently leaning into their monitors. They had always been the ones asking the most questions and seemed to genuinely care about what I had to say. The other students had signed up just because they wanted an easy elective. *Easy. Great writing is not easy. It's terribly hard work with a beautifully exhausting outcome.*

"Everyone has trauma," I say. "I want you to make a list of different types of trauma that people face."

"And?"

"And you create a fictional character for each type."

"How does that relate to writing our memoir?"

"Ask yourself how you would react to someone else's trauma. Describe what their pain feels like."

"But we don't know any pain but our own."

"Exactly. Empathy is learned. Empathy is crucial to writing a bestselling memoir. Think of every person in your life and how their flaws and trauma have shaped who you have become."

"Your techniques have gotten boring, Byrne."

"Just the two of you left," I say, taking a sip of my juice box. "I think we're about done with the class."

"Forever?"

"I'll be around. If you have any questions you can send an email."

"But what if we get stuck? I always get writer's block."

"Email, Caden."

"But I need to—"

Blank screen. Their faces abruptly disappear. *Class over.* The blackouts have reached their part of the city.

I spin in my chair, working to make myself dizzy.... to throw myself into another dimension. Away from this. I'm gonna miss those kids. It's not getting any better. Our power will be cut soon too. I know it.

"Byrne." Rosiegirl taps on my door. "Can I write with you? I made you another rope bracelet."

"Another?"

"You can layer it with the others."

I glance down at my left arm. I have six jewel tone bracelets all made from her yarn scraps. Also have two leather ones on the right wrist. Never was into adorning myself with such things before meeting her.

"Wait a sec. I'll be right there."

One of my new favorite pastimes is practicing my cursive. Rosiegirl does it with me sometimes, and I'm pretty sure it's because she loves using my chalkboard. Chalkboards are obsolete according to her...which apparently makes me an old dude.

"Byrne, you're thirty-three right?"

"Yep."

"So, you must've grown up learning cursive in school."

"Hardly. Wasn't long before things changed. But you're twenty-seven. You would've known about cursive too."

"Only by watching old shows. I like signing my name that way, but I can't write full sentences in cursive."

"Try it."

Xavedean and Rosiegirl. Riding a war horse together through a burning forest. She's wilder than me. More daring. Such a free spirit.

"Byrne?" Rosiegirl's backing up as I write words across her cursive. "Byrne, that's my sentence."

We got this. We're charging onto the field. I love your hair in the wind, Rosiegirl. Your strong legs in the fight.

"Hey, Byrne. You good?"

My piece of chalk hits the floor. I look at her. *Shoot.* "Sorry. I'm sorry. I was just…"

"Yeah. One of those magical writer places."

I have several go-to character voices that I use when talking to Rosiegirl. One is the burly hero Xavedean in my book series Warrior Run, the I'm-cooler-than-you pop star Envious Sky voice, my suave, crooning Scottish horseman Jak MacEaldan voice, and the wine-sipping, snobby anti-hero Codymak. It's often during our script-reading sessions where I like bouncing between Envious Sky and Codymak. I love altering my vocal tone and inflection just to make people laugh. And yes, Rosiegirl and I write our own epic skit scripts for passing the time when bored. They never make any sense which makes it all the more awesome to act out. I love being goofy with her.

"I wish I had your imagination," she says. "It's a beautiful thing to think like that."

Beautiful. I smile. She thinks I have a beautiful mind. "Well, most people call it eccentric or quirky."

"Actually I like the word eccentric too. It has a sciency ring to it. Like…you're a creator of worlds, an inventor of characters, and an eccentric artist with a pencil. Or chalk."

"Yeah. Eccentric artist with chalk. Writer's chalk."

"Yeah."

I freeze in my head. *Why's she looking at me like that? Floating hearts, stomach flips, darn it I feel like vomiting. What's going on? Her cuteness is overwhelming my body that much? What's wrong with you, Byrne? Relax! You're a grown man. Use your wisdom! Shoot. Actually…I think I just ran out of it. Running on dork juice now. Potent stuff.*

"You good?"

"Yeah." I scrawl one more word on the board while looking back at her. "I'm good, Rosiegirl."

Coward.

Six

Passing The Time

Saturday June 28th, 2025 5:50 PM

Cameras see everything in and out of Tower 881. No freedom of movement. We can still receive mail, grocery deliveries, and gifts from those on the outside, but that blessing comes with a huge caveat. Every few nights they raid our building. I've never heard a reason for why they destroy certain apartments or why they beat up certain residents, but I try my best to stay in line. Even then...I get assaulted just the same as everyone else. We all have bruises, black eyes, broken noses, welts.

I can barely throw a proper punch or kick, but once in awhile I create a wild scene of my own in the corridor. If I hear them beating up on one of the kids, I'm sprinting to put myself in their place.

Being caught outside after hours is usually a death sentence. The siren goes off and we all know someone's under siege. But during the day it's safe to be out of the building. As long as it's

35

on the roof or at the First Checkpoint. The official curfew for us is 11 PM to 6 AM. The noise ordinance is from 10 PM to 6 AM. And forget about trying to break those rules…there's a nasty consequence for everything done wrong.

We're only human. Not extraterrestrials. Not robots. Only human. Why do corporate big dogs prioritize AI over human life? It's not fair. Old school living is just as good. Primal is beautiful.

"You're cheating, Cinnamon."

"Am not."

"I can totally see the cards you failed to put down."

"I got nothing."

"You got a pair."

I'm sitting in the corridor of the fifteenth floor, congealed bowl of instant noodles balanced on my legs, watching four of the goofiest women play a made-up card game. The brunette with the caterpillar hair clip, Lyrical, has a habit of holding back her cards. I haven't yet figured out the rules to it yet, but when I do come up with my noodles and sweaty, shaggy hair, all four of them immediately pause their game to see who can greet me the loudest.

"Wanna play, Storyteller?"

"Nope. I'm gonna go play with Dingo in a few minutes. He says he wants me to steer a pirate ship into dangerous waters."

Melancholy, the silver hair diva, smashes her cigarette into the carpet. "I thought that kid like wolves."

"Well, I like wolves too. I think it's because I started him on it," I say. I stand, taking my bowl with me, and walk carefully around the cigarette butt. I've burned my feet too many times from people dropping their smokes in the building…none of the smokers will quit, especially not now with how worse it's getting. But I guess I understand it. We all need to cope.

6:20 PM

It turns out that Dingo changed his mind from wanting to play pirates to watching *Peter Pan* on a tiny video player. *Kids. Always something new.*

"Rosiegirl made brownies for you and Dingo," I say to Pardon. I put the plate on the counter.

"Tell her thanks," he grunts. "Wanna watch the game with me?"

I look at the already-played baseball game on the screen. "No thanks. I'm just hanging with Dingo."

Pardon gets up and takes the whole plate of brownies for himself. "The kid's name is Kaleb."

"Dingo," I whisper as I sit with Dingo on the other side of the apartment. We are on the cool kitchen floor, ducked down by the sink on the little guy's mattress.

"Hey boss," Pardon suddenly calls out. "You kiss Rosiegirl yet?"

It takes a minute to realize what he just asked. "No."

"You should. Everyone knows you like her."

"Word spreads fast," I mumble to myself. "She might not want me the same way."

"Just make a move, Story."

"I don't want to freak her out."

"It'll never happen then," he says. "Coward."

"Kiss her and get married," Dingo says while staring at his screen. The swagger in his little kid voice makes me laugh.

"Think so?"

"Get her, boss," he says, imitating his uncle.

"Well, maybe," I say. "But, Pardon, I really think you should do that eagle flying scenario I told you about. It's fun."

"Nope," Pardon says. "That's for you and Kaleb to do. I don't pretend to be nothing."

All right. All right, Byrne. Not everyone gets the hype of imagination. Just let him be.

Seven

Imagination Therapy

9:09 PM

Imagination Therapy is an off-the-wall something that I came up with. A twice-a-week event in my apartment where any resident can come and release their fears, frustrations, and gripes under the guise of making up stories. Rosiegirl says that the way I operate it reminds her of Drama Class in high school.

Today's prelude involved her standing by my open door and cheerily telling everyone to put on name tags as they came in. It's usually the same six residents joining us, and I knew that the two old men, Barnowl and Wicket, would be grumbling like clogged garbage disposals the second they saw the name tags. But it turns out that the homemade muffins she had set out as the therapeutic snack proved an immediate appeasement for the old-timers.

"Does anybody need any soda? There's still coffee too."

"I'll take the watery concoction," Wicket says to Rosiegirl.

The way she looks in her blue tank top, sweeping yellow skirt, barefoot in flashy gold toe rings…*wow. Always wow.* I bite my lip, internally scolding my wandering eyes. *Byrne, just stop. Chill. But just look at Rosiegirl.* Carrying the coffee pot through the kitchen nook and circling it around the nine of us, including little Dingo who swears he's allowed to have just one more cup.

"You mean the watery concoction, buddy," Wicket mumbles into his mug. "Dagnabbers, it's always hot!"

"Dagnabbers!" Dingo echoes and sips the tiny amount that Rosiegirl has just poured him.

I smile. It takes way too long to get things going some nights. Well, day or night it can be a drag of a prelude to the actual storytelling. That's where I'm at my best. When I'm free to be as whimsical as I want.

Some residents don't have an imagination at all and get mad at me for spouting my stories. I try to avoid those ones entirely. But I get to help the eager ones use their own minds to escape into fantasy worlds. They scoffed at my techniques at first but now the mood seems giddy when I lead everyone into a story scenario. Things quickly fly out of control when Sportscar and Aviator butt heads over who has the more sensible story idea.

"What's in your castle, Aviator?" I ask.

"Glazed doughnuts and panda bears."

"That doesn't make sense," Sportscar says.

"Doesn't have to make sense," I say as I pace the room, eyes still closed. It took ten minutes to get Grandma Ursa to let go of my hand so that I could do my usual walk around the circle, and I was glad that Rosiegirl jumped in to give her someone to hold onto. I prefer having everyone sit on the floor in a circle when we trade stories. It's centering, calming, and gives me the satisfaction of being a teacher again.

I've learned that sometimes to connect with the broken minds, I have to lean into their unstable ramblings. Grandma Ursa is one of the most elderly residents and she says I look like her dead grandson. I hear it every time she comes to therapy. Always has to hold my hand and offer a back scratch because her grandson liked them. I gave up turning down the back scratches because I found that she does it anyway. Rosiegirl thinks her connection with me is hilarious.

"Okay," I say. "Dingo, would you like a turn making up the story?"

"Yes!" He jumps to his feet, sending his cup flying, and like a secret agent stopping the timer before the bomb, I save the drink container from touching the floor. *Yeah, random. This is a writer's life. No judgment here.*

Rosiegirl giggles when I take Dingo's place in the circle. She's in a very bubbly mood tonight.

"So, there's this baby whale that needs help climbing waffles! We have to push him up! Come on! Baby whale!"

Everyone else is looking insanely confused by the scenario, but I'm enthralled. I love when things don't make sense. It's a story time. Why not let the youngest one in the room take charge and make us feel like a kid too?

"Stand up, Story!" Dingo yells. "Run from the lion!"

"Lions again?"

"Yes!! We all have to run on the water!"

So we all run in place from the lion who somehow is chasing us across a vast ocean. Dingo doesn't tell us to stop. Then he says for us to spin around for a thousand minutes because the lion won't catch us when we're in a zoomy circle.

"Boy, I'm gonna throw up!" Wicket announces in the midst

of his rickety spinning.

Rosiegirl is cracking up as she twirls and bumps into Dingo who then tells us to hop up and down because we're on a trampoline in the desert.

"How did a desert get here?" Aviator asks. He rolls his eyes with Sportscar but they both keep playing the game.

Grandma Ursa's back to holding my hand again, so now as I try to follow along in little Dingo's wild story, I also have to help Ursa move with me. She's just silently grinning as I take her along on our adventure. The room is sticky and sweaty like a rainforest now from all this activity.

"Dingo," I say.

"What?"

"Tell me there's a resting spot in the desert soon."

"There is!" He points to the front door and yells in the loudest voice possible: "CLASS DISMISS!"

Rosiegirl drops to the floor laughing harder than I've ever seen her laugh. The two young guys, two old guys, and Grandma Ursa just look confused as anything.

"Okay." I raise my hand. "Okay, we can end it early."

"Bye, Story!" Dingo says before zooming out the door and straight back into his apartment.

Tell me that's not the most random thing ever. Well...I can't. I can't because I'm a writer and I can still top what Dingo just did.

"Best therapy ever," Rosiegirl says.

I'm worn out by Dingo for sure, but kids always make things more fun. I have to agree with her.

10:31 PM

I can feel Rosiegirl staring at my back. She watches me write down notes after everyone leaves, probably wondering why I stand holding a piece of paper against the wall when I could just be sitting. Her eyes are burning a hole through me. I bet she's silently hoping I'll turn around.

"Do you need me to help with anything else?"

"No."

"Okay. I'll take the muffin tray and props back to my apartment."

"Okay," I say with my back still turned.

"Why don't you write the idea down on the chalkboard? It's right there."

"I need to hold a pencil for this one."

"Okay. Good night, Byrne."

I'm in the middle of a thought so I can't respond, but I hear her slowly walk to the door. I end up on a writing streak with chalk dust all over me by the time curfew arrives, and I catch the sound of an oncoming raid.

Oh no. They're hitting up our floor.

I flip the chalkboard round to the other side and furiously start scribbling my name in cursive. *It's relaxing. I'm scared.* I don't want anyone to know that I'm scared.

A scream. I drop the chalk.

A familiar scream.

They're in Rosiegirl's apartment.

Eight

The Raid

11:15 PM

"That's my jewelry stuff! Hey!"

"Don't fight back, 086."

"Where you taking my stuff? Hey! That's my cereal!"

"It may be contaminated."

"And what are you going to do with it? Test it? Share it?" Rosiegirl's sounding angrily sarcastic. She doesn't get that way with anyone else except… "It's mine! Never got stupid plague or anything!"

"Don't insult us, 086. Mage, take her out."

NO.

"Get off me! Stop! That's my stuff! Stop it!"

I open my door and wait in the corridor, knowing what's coming.

"Stop it! Let go of me!"

They violently drag her out of her apartment and shove her

44

into the wall.

"Rosiegirl!" I'm shoved just as hard when I intervene. I look down at the floor to avoid my face being struck with their metal disciplinarian rods. Everyone can hear the assault from inside their apartments, but no one does anything. Because they can't.

Rosiegirl gets up, wipes blood from her lip, and screams hoarsely as the rest of the Oficialkers walk out of her trashed apartment. "Find anything, you crazies?!"

They give her a stern look but don't attack us again.

I wait to see if they're going into Dingo's apartment before following Rosiegirl back into hers. The raid is moving up to the next floor.

"Second time. Second time they hit me like that." Rosiegirl sits in the middle of her ruined projects, wincing as she presses a hand to her jaw.

"You okay?"

"Better than my jewelry."

"Yeah."

"You're hurt too, Byrne."

"Yeah. I'm okay."

"I'm okay too."

"I won't be able to sleep now," I say. "Adrenaline."

"Me too."

We look at each other, noting on our bodies they had beat us up. "I'll have bruises all over my arms and back," I say. "Your face will be swollen."

"It's okay." She's good at shrugging off terrifying experiences. "I got ice."

I wish I could cuddle her. She did nothing to deserve this.

"What did I do to them?" she asks.

"Nothing." *You did nothing bad.* "They're just evil, Rosiegirl."

"People like us shouldn't have to fight."

"What are you talking about?" I change my voice to Warrior Run's burly hero Xavedean, doing my best to lighten the mood. "You and me are made to fight, little chrysalis."

She smiles. Blushes.

"'And they did not hide,'" I dramatically quote my book's passage. "'They stood as they had desired. Furious, strong, ready to defend the House of Kinbeare. Oaths taken and true...'" I trail off and smile as Rosiegirl continues the passage..."'She was more than his shield maiden. Wild to fight. Wild to stand with him in death and tears.'"

"'And they ran to the war,'" we finish together. "'And the monsters could not win. They could not take them to darkness.'"

"You know my story so well," I say.

"It's my favorite book series. Of anything I've ever read."

I want to kiss her so badly as she leans in and stares into my eyes. "You don't give yourself enough credit, Byrne."

"Imagination is survival," I say.

She puts her arms around me. Sighs. Shaky breaths. She's exhausted. I hug her back, rubbing strands of her messy hair between my fingers. *I got you, elvish princess.*

I'm exhausted too. But happy to hold her. Happy to hold Rosiegirl.

Nine

Morning

Sunday June 29th, 2025 7:47 AM

"Byrne, you made the English muffin wrong."

"How did I do that?"

"You didn't put butter in the crevices before layering the strawberry jam."

"Butter doesn't taste good on English muffins."

"It does. It's my new breakfast food."

"Since when?"

"I ate two of them at four in the morning."

Every time I join Rosiegirl for breakfast I wish I could gently kiss her. She's got such a glow in the mornings. The cutest summer pajamas…turquoise tank top and matching soft shorts. "Any progress on the steampunk earrings?"

"Nope."

"Why? Trouble with attaching the mini gears?"

She doesn't answer the question. Slides the bottom half of

47

her English muffin toward me. "Try it the right way, Byrne."

I bite into it. "Very good," I say.

She grins, takes our empty cups to the sink, and I watch her do a little dance as she rinses them.

"Rosiegirl, would you be mad if I called you baby?"

"What?"

Stupid. Why? Pretend you didn't say that, Byrne. You. Did. Not. "Sorry. No, nevermind."

"No, what did you say?"

"Forget it."

"You wanna call me a pet name?"

"All my character voices have special names for you. They call you things like 'fluttering dove' and 'sugar sunshine'. I think Maddox Byrne should have a special name for you too."

"Rosiegirl. You call me that. I like it."

I smile. *I'm so dumb.* And consider banging my head on the counter. "Fair enough, princess," I mumble.

"But you can make up anything you want for me. Another character? Who else do I look like in your books?"

No one else. She looks like my dream woman. Period.

"What if you wrote a new book and I was a unicorn queen? That'd be cool."

"You're too beautiful for that," I say. "You're the aurora borealis come to Earth."

"But unicorns are beautiful."

Wow. I dropped a massive compliment and she didn't even blink.

"I mean, Byrne, what girl hasn't dreamed of being a unicorn or riding on one? You're not a girl, so you wouldn't know. Just saying that I love unicorns."

"Okay. Sure. Unicorns. A unicorn queen named..." I rest my chin on my hands, staring at her. *I can't think. My brain just farted.*

"Oh! Oh!" She jumps up and down. "Lightning Blue! You can call me Lightning Blue!"

I love her excitement. *What a goofy, childish, amazing human.* "Lightning Blue? What about a name with a purple hue in it?"

"No." She shakes her head. "I don't need any color besides blue if I'm a unicorn queen."

Our conversation almost always deviates like a roller coaster on strong coffee. I'm sure that my own mind is what makes her dive off track, but even when she gets on a roll about some other topic, she never seems to care or get upset that she forgot what we were talking about before.

Best friends. That's what makes us best friends.

Ten

No More Light

〜∞〜

Monday June 30th, 2025 9:15 PM

The blackout finally happened…two hours before sunset. Rather anticlimactic if you ask me. But now the kids are starting to notice the darkness and are getting scared. Every appliance is down. Every phone, computer, tablet, and television is blank. Rosiegirl and I are going to each apartment door and asking if the kids want to play flashlight tag on the roof. I know it's wasteful to use flashlights for a game…but we have to do something to help them have fun. *It's going to get worse.*

Eight-year-old Lilac's mom Bellawise is sobbing against her fridge, a bottle of wine and a cigarette in hand. Lilac looks confused as to why her mom is completely fallen apart…I still don't judge anyone. Even when they're cracking under the pressure. I just try to make the kids feel safe.

Rosiegirl gently offers her hand and Lilac comes with us.

"You like tag?" I ask.

"Yeah. I'm the best at tag."

"What about flashlight tag?"

"Yeah. I'm best at that too."

"So am I!" Dingo says. He spins in forward circles instead of walking normally.

"How are you going to make it up that stairs like that?" Rosiegirl asks.

"I can do it. Spinning works good."

"I can spin too!" Lilac says.

We make it to the roof with nine kids, each one of us holding a working flashlight. The game of tag starts innocently, but I notice Rosiegirl is nervous while watching the kids run close to the edges. Thirty stories up. We have to look out for the little ones as they burn off their energy.

"Magic up here," she says. She's looking at the stars.

"It is."

"Maybe the blackout isn't so bad. Get to see the stars clearly without all the city lights."

"You can always find joy in something," I say.

We listen to the kids laughing as they wave their flashlights around. The tag game seems to have died down, and now they are all pretending to be superheroes. They're having fun. Happy. Their voices are so gleeful.

"You really add joy to their world, Byrne," Rosiegirl says.

"It's the only way to survive," I say. "I want them to keep living. To see the end of this."

"Well, I can't imagine when they'll let us go back to normal."

"I know. But I'll never run out of ideas to distract them. Just keep telling stories. Making up games. Be goofy."

"Yeah," she says, grinning in the erratic trails of light beams. "You're good at that."

Stories. Pretending. Pretending everything is fine when it's not. That is a gift. I didn't used to believe in myself and what I could bring to people. But now I do. I have to. Imagination is survival...it has to be.

Eleven

Pretending

Tuesday July 1st, 2025 11:00 AM

A chef and an orchestra conductor. That is today's Imagination Therapy. I'm pretending to cook a fantastic meal for Rosiegirl since we don't have a working stove or microwave... courtesy of the blackout. She's already laughing at me as I strut around with an invisible tray of hors d'oeuvre. It's just the two of us playing the pretending game.

"Ma'am, would you care for a bacon-wrapped scallop?"

"I would love one, Mr. Waiter."

"I'm not a waiter. I'm a chef-conductor."

"Oh, forgive me. This is a new role for you."

I try to keep a serious face but can't. *Mr. Waiter? Hmm. Would that be interesting in a new book series? It could be about a waiter who wants to be a chef who wants to be a conductor and his girlfriend is a classical pianist.*

"Byrne, I thought I was supposed to be the orchestra conductor."

"I don't see any conducting," I say. *Rabbit trail! Time to deviate from the current scenario.*

Rosiegirl seems to read my mind and immediately twirls around like she's wearing a princess dress. "Dance with me," she says. "We're at a Victorian club."

I take her hand and we dance to silent music. All we need now is some wine. I realize Victorian clubs aren't a thing, but if it is in Rosiegirl's mind…it's real.

The dancing evolves into a flirty sword fight and then into a singing competition between her and my character Envious Sky. Neither of us can sing well. *Our voices break glass. Ha. Ha.*

"Hey. I'm gonna use some of my computer battery to watch *Prince Of Egypt.*"

"Okay." I'm used to her always wanting to watch that movie. It figures she would have saved some of the juice in her laptop before the blackout. It's super cute because she always cries at the same three parts in it.

Story idea….new one…hmm…maybe a thriller with the waiter and the girlfriend pianist. She gets kidnapped by a secret vampire society and then…wait. Oh! His name is Starbarn and her name is Windmagic.

"Byrne, you're mixing fantasy names with modern thriller scenarios, aren't you?"

"How can you tell?"

"You have a face for that. Your eyes go trance-like and you tilt your head when in fantasy-name mode."

I see her grinning me at me when I look over my shoulder. I'm busy scrawling things on the chalkboard. "You like that?"

"Yeah, it's cute."

YES. I love when she says I'm cute. I mean what I did was cute.

I'm not cute. No, I am. What I do is what I am. Ugh. Byrne...get yourself together.

2:49 PM

"Pardon jumped!"

"On the roof! Dingo saw the whole thing!"

Rosiegirl turns down the volume on her laptop.

"Why's no one up there? The kid's alone on the roof?"

The commotion is right outside my door.

"He'll jump too!"

"The kid's still up there!"

I look at Rosiegirl. She's reaching out to me, opening her mouth to form words. "Go get him, Byrne," she says.

But I barely hear her.

I'm already running.

Twelve

Jumper

3:31 PM

This time when I run up the stairs…when I run to Dingo…
there's no music in my head. No violin. No drums. No piano.
I just hear my own breathing. I hear myself breaking. Dingo.
He's alone. I have to move faster. The traumatized person in
me wants to fade into my imaginary world. But the protector
in me just wants Dingo to be all right. *It can't get any worse than
this. It can't.*

He's standing near the edge. Looking out at the cityscape.
Not looking down. *Please. Please, don't look down.* I drop to a
knee and try to say his name, but a sob comes out instead. I
cover my mouth with my arm and try to compose myself before
whispering, "Dingo."

He doesn't move.

"Dingo."

He's still looking at the sky. His tiny body looks like it could topple off the edge any second. I come forward, saying his name every few steps. I crouch at the roof's edge next to him. "Buddy, c'mon."

Finally he looks at me and I see glazed eyes.

"He said he could fly. He wanted to fly, Story."

"C'mere, Dingo. I got you." I stretch out my arms. "C'mere. Let's go downstairs."

"He wanted to fly away."

"I know. I know." I blink back a torrent of tears, feeling my glasses slide down my nose. "C'mon, buddy."

He stretches his arms out, mimicking me, eyes looking down. A broken little boy.

"It's not okay," I whisper. "I'm so sorry, Dingo."

Dingo clings tightly to me when I pick him up, and I have nothing else to say except, "It's not okay. I know, buddy. It's not." *Nobody should want to do that but they do. They do, buddy.* "I'm so sorry. I'm sorry. It's not okay. You're not okay." I walk us back to the stairs and he starts to sob, his tears and sweat dampening my shirt. "I got you, buddy. I got you. You're with me, Dingo." I comfort him all the way down to our floor, fighting the shakes in my legs.

The journey down the corridor feels longer than it's ever been. Everyone is standing outside their doors to watch me walk by. Their faces are sullen, scared, angry. *What did I do?*

"Story," Wildride says. "They're saying you caused his death. You made him jump."

I shift Dingo to my other shoulder as he continues to sob and refuses to be set down. "What?"

"All your talk about flying like a bird messed him up. Made him crazy."

"Yeah, Story," Tenor the Food Bringer says. "You help none

of us. None of us in this place. All you talk is death scenarios and stupid fantasy."

"I've never talked about death. I'm just trying to help—"

"Your stories didn't help him," Wildride says. I can tell that he's been drinking. Been smoking. He leans close to me, spitting in my face when he screams, "Your imagination is shit!"

"They do help," Rosiegirl says. She comes to me, silently convinces Dingo to be carried by her, and stares down Wildride and Tenor. "Leave Byrne alone. All of you let him be."

It takes way too long for the residents to go back inside their apartments. I'm on the edge of crying in sympathy with Dingo.

"Don't listen to him, Byrne."

"I was just trying to help."

"You are." Rosiegirl waits for me to unlock my door and follows behind with Dingo. "Here, buddy," she says to him. "I'll get you a juice box."

The juice is all warm and disgusting now in the powerless fridge. Dingo's not going to drink that.

"You'll stay with Story, okay? You'll sleep here."

Dingo hiccups and downs the entire juice box in twelve seconds. He put his face on Rosiegirl's sleeve, getting her sticky with his tears and sweat. She looks up at me from the floor and mouths for me to get a damp washcloth.

Okay. I use a water ration to wet one and bring it to her, sitting on the other side of Dingo. Poor buddy is so hot that it almost feels like he's got a fever. I cool him down with the washcloth, wishing the power could come back on just for twenty minutes…just enough time for a happy video clip on the internet.

Anything to make this little guy's terror disappear. He saw what I didn't want him to see. What no one should see. He saw his uncle jump.

Thirteen

Dorky And Awkward

10:15 PM

"Why do people get angry when I'm just trying to help?"

"I know." Rosiegirl touches my shoulder, sitting down next to me. We look at where Dingo's sleeping on the floor. He refused to be on anything other than a red sleeping bag. "Don't hate yourself, Byrne."

"He's traumatized. He watched him fall."

"It'll be okay."

I want to just enjoy her body being close to mine, but I keep thinking about Dingo. What he saw. What he heard. "He'll cry in the night."

"I know. You'll be there for him."

"Yeah." *So many things. So many scenarios. What-ifs. Always the what-ifs. Is that just a writer thing?*

"Well hey, I'm gonna get some sleep, but I'll bring you some cheese crackers in the morning."

"Thank you. Thanks, Rosie." I want to kiss Rosiegirl as she stands and heads for the door, but I chew on my lip instead. She looks angelic with the messy red hair and sympathetic brown eyes. "Sweet dreams, love dove," I whisper, half-hoping that she doesn't hear me.

She turns around and smiles. "Sweet dreams to you too. Don't let the nightmares win."

"Okay," I say.

She's hesitating at the door. I can hear it creaking.

Say something else, Byrne. She likes you. I think she really, really likes you. I'm asking her. Ask her, Byrne. "Wanna go on a date?"

"What?" she says.

I drop my head fast and my glasses tumble to the floor. I bend to pick them up, but her hand is already there. "A date. You can dress up fancy if you want. Or not. I'll ask Alchemist and Everwhen to watch Dingo for awhile. And maybe I can find batteries for my old Discman."

"You have a Discman?"

"I do. Somewhere in one of my drawers."

"And you want us to have a date with your Discman on the roof?"

"Yeah. We can share headphones. Take turns." *Romantic to me. Maybe it sounds really dorky for a guy to think of that.*

We look at each other as I put my glasses back on. She's grinning, head tilted. "Sure, Byrne. We can go on a date. Although, I think the time we've spent together already counts as dates too."

Dagnabbers. Yes, I'm stealing the word from Wicket. My face is hot. "Yeah." *Stupid Byrne. Duuuude. She counts all the other times hanging out as real dates. She likes me already to call that dating. Wow.*

"You don't mind canned ravioli, do you? I'll bring some for dinner tomorrow night."

"Sure, Rosiegirl. I love food from a can."

"Okay. It's a date." She smiles as she exits my apartment, and I breathe out hard, hands running through my hair. I feel so stupid. I'm like a teenager inside and I'm in my thirties. I've hardly had any good experiences with love or dates or wooing a woman, yet here's the one I want the most…and she's as chill as an ice age polar bear.

Make it memorable, Byrne. Up your imagination game. Be cool. No. Be weird. Be so amazingly weird and quirky to match her quirky.

Fourteen

Rosiegirl Says...

———✦———

Wednesday July 2nd, 2025 6:45 PM

Our date on the rooftop includes three of my favorite things. Rosiegirl in a yellow halter top and denim shorts, cold ravioli in a can, and a set of eight candles lit with a bear-shaped cigarette lighter borrowed from Alchemist. The ravioli is mostly gone, and now we are acting out scenes from my books.

"It's the scene where Rosiegirl watches Xavedean duel his nemesis while riding dragons over a river."

"She doesn't have any lines in that one though."

I do a little shuffle dance while thinking for a moment. "Oh! You can act out the part where she runs and jumps over rocks and tree branches to keep up with them."

"Byrne," Rosiegirl says, "I can't run and jump carelessly on this roof."

"You saw the kids doing it the other night. And you know that Rosiegirl is a little bit reckless in the series." I step closer to her, grinning at the satin blanket around her shoulders. *Her makeshift cloak.* "You are, in fact, a little wild one."

She spins away from me, throwing off her cloak. Suddenly is holding an imaginary sword. "How about if Rosiegirl duels Xavedean instead? She shouldn't have to watch him have all the fun."

"Oh? You want to fight me, do you?" I say in Xavedean's burly voice.

"I absolutely do," she says with a grin. "Come get me, Xave."

We pretend fight, circling each other, ducking and diving under our swords. She's so graceful when acting goofy with me. It's even more romantic that we're running around barefoot in the humid night air...*like rogue warriors in a forest. Or fairies. I'm the big, muscular type. An anomaly in the fairy world. She is as all fairies should be. Delicate, feisty, stunning hair and sharp eyes.* But it's a rooftop in a big city. In a lockdown. Trapped. But under the stars it feels free. Stars always feel free. And beautiful. She and I are so breathtaking under the night sky.

"Byrne? You lost again?"

"Sorry. How long you been saying my name?"

"Just said it once." She smiles. "Don't worry. I'm not bothered by your daydreaming."

"I'm sorry. I'm the one who asked you up here. I should pay more attention."

"It's okay. You're really..."

"I'm really what?"

Rosiegirl suddenly dips her head and backs away.

What? What's she trying to say?

"I think I love you."

"What?"

"I think I love you, Byrne."

My ears must be broken. They have to be. I stutter in my response. *Rosiegirl loves...* "Are you sure?"

She nods.

"Really?"

She nods again. "Yes."

I lean in.

She's standing still. Letting me come closer. Letting me breathe on her lips.

"Don't jinx it," she whispers.

"I'm not," I whisper back.

"We're gonna jinx it."

"We won't."

She looks from my eyes to my mouth. Back to my eyes. "Byrne—"

And I kiss her.

7:21 PM

One one thousand. Two one thousand. Three one thousand.

"Byrne." She leans away, her fingers running through my hair. Looking down and breathing soft, she whispers, "Don't die too."

She's thinking of her last love. Worried I will be lost the same way. *Imagination is survival. But nothing is for certain.*

"We're alive." I draw her back to me, stroking her cheek. I'm trying not to be giddy, but I can't be normal right now. *We just had our first kiss.* "We're alive, warrior princess," I say in my Jak MacEaldan voice.

"For now," she says.

"We're alive," I repeat.

"You're so strange, Byrne." There's a whimper at the end of her words...as if she's forcing herself to not give into a firework of emotions.

"Well," I say with a shrug, "I'm a writer so...."

She half-smiles, laying her head against my chest, and squeezes me in a hard embrace.

"I promise I'm not going anywhere," I say.

"Men always make impossible promises."

"I'm not going anywhere." *Never stop repeating it.* Now that she's expressed her feelings for me, I won't stop saying how much I want her. "I'm not going anywhere, Rosiegirl. I love you."

"No character voice. No costume." She stares at my face. "You're just you."

"Just me," I say.

"I love your strangeness."

"I love yours too." She tilts her head to the side and smiles. I bet she's thinking about the kiss. I go in for another, cupping her chin in my hands, pressing my body to hers. She lets me pull her down to the ground. We lay next to each other.

"Byrne..."

"Love dove."

"Byrne."

"You're my magic," I whisper in her ear.

"Byrne," she says between kisses, "you're a warrior poet."

"That good?"

"Yeah. But..." She turns her head from my mouth and hurriedly sits up. "I have jewelry to finish."

Okay. Chill, Byrne. Slow it down.

She's rubbing her arms on the places where my hands wandered. Little quivering breaths lift her chest and shoulders.

*She's not ready for...I'm not...I mean I am but...*I push my glasses back up. I'm shaking. *Rosiegirl needs space.* She deserves time to think it through. And she deserves honor. Respectable honor. But I love her like crazy. She's so beautiful.

"Okay. Okay, Rosiegirl. I'll let you get back to your project." But I stay close when I sit up beside her, moving in to kiss her cheek, lips, neck. "But I'll be next door." *As always. We can always talk. My real life princess.*

"I know," she whispers. She kisses me back, grabs my hair. "I know you are."

Rosiegirl. I smile as she lingers, clearly enjoying the attention. And she HAS my full attention. I'm wild for her. *I want you to know that, love dove.*

"You're always there to talk with me, Byrne. I love it."

"Me too." *I love everything about you.*

Fifteen

To War

Thursday July 3rd, 2025 9:40 PM

I put out the memo that anyone is welcome to come for a therapy session tonight. Dingo's sitting with Rosiegirl, munching on stale animal crackers, and I'm pacing between them and Wicket, Adorbs, and Silvercrown. I hold a single sheet of paper, reading aloud the scenario. It's about war. An old war for old, tired people. But in this scenario, the people have one last ounce of courage in their hearts.

The story is meant to bring about a war cry in this room. A cry to release all negative emotion......I know it sounds silly to everyone who is not born with my vivid imagination. I know it is pointless to try to stir up a cause to shout when all are lethargic and depressed. But the point, in my mind, is that we try to survive. That we try to make do with what we got right here. Right now.

When I'm not consumed with thoughts of Rosiegirl, I'm

consumed with my passion for storytelling. And using it to live. To help others live. Even if it's just one more day or one more minute on Earth.

I find myself staring at Rosiegirl as I speak the lines of dialogue that I wrote into the scenario. She's hugging Dingo, holding him as if he was her son. She smiles. I notice that Wicket, Adorbs, and Silvercrown are giving us weird looks. They know we're a couple now. We're probably making them sick with our goofy heart eyes.

"We stand to win. Stand to fight. Stand to call out the enemy and raise a wild freedom. If we cannot show courage in the darkness, how do we thrive? How do we make them hear us? Warriors stand tall. Warriors scream when they run forward. Not a fight but a last defense. A last defense for all those who came before. Howl with me, brethren. Make them hear our cries."

"To war!" Rosiegirl says, lifting an arm over her head.

Dingo raises his arms in solidarity, an animal cracker stuffed in his mouth. No clue what's being said, but includes himself anyway. *I love this little guy. Bravery in a kid is like nothing else I've ever seen. Strong before his time. Little warrior.*

"War cry!" I shout. "Howl!"

"Howl!" Dingo echoes, starting to yip and bark like a wolf.

I fling my head back, howling like I do on the roof.

Rosiegirl doesn't howl. Neither do the other three in the room.

"C'mon!" I encourage. "Let them hear us! Freedom! Run wild and fast! The world is ours to win!"

Dingo gets up and runs to me, hugging my legs as we howl together. I lift him up in my arms and smile. "You got it, little wolf. You know how to sing to the night."

"Yeah! I sing like them!"

"You do."

Everyone else is quiet. I can see Rosiegirl thinking about doing it too, but she stays quiet. Her eyes are teary. Emotional. I can't figure out if it's because she's moved by me and Dingo's wolf howling or if she's just feeling overwhelmed by the thought of war.

"You can go," I say to the others. I know they're mentally checked out. *And I need some more alone time with my girl.*

10:01 PM

Alchemist and Everwhen are kind enough to watch Dingo again while I take a walk with Rosiegirl. The corridors are pitch black. No lights anywhere. No fans. No sounds. We hold hands on the way up the stairs, and she doesn't seem nervous at all this time. Not nervous to be on the roof in the middle of the night.

"Let's go look at the stars," I whisper.

"I'm with you," she says. "I love the night sky."

"Me too." *It's paradise.*

"It's freedom up there, isn't it?"

"It is."

"Like flying."

"Yes." I squeeze her hand tight. "Like flying."

Sixteen

Turning The Page

10:48 PM

"I hope someone tells our story."

"What story?"

"How we met," she says. "All your character voices. How you thought I looked like your book's heroine."

I hold her tight, rocking her against my chest as we look up at the stars. "You are my Rosiegirl."

"I'm glad." She breathes lightly, drawing my attention back to her eyes. "I wouldn't want to be here without you, Byrne."

The curfew is coming and I don't care. I'm with my precious girl.

I gently kiss her as the sirens blare around us. Her lips taste like spearmint. Soft, warm breath. Fiery tingles on skin. *This is the dream come alive.*

"Just turning the page, right?" she whispers.

"Yeah," I say. "We're turning the page."

The Horn of Aermad.

And the sound of...Rosiegirl smiles at me and I smile back.

Howling. The residents of Tower 881 are all leaning out their windows howling like wolves.

"That's for us," she says. "For you, Storyteller Byrne."

"War cry."

"Our war cry."

Should we join them?

I see the mischief in her eyes and she nods at my thought. *Freedom.*

AWOOOOOOOOOO.

Everything's going to be okay. Even if it's not. It's going to be okay.

Trust me.

I'm a writer.

About the Author

Han M Greenbarg has been in love with writing fiction since childhood. She is an avid coffee drinker, proud dog mom, and lover of country music and war movies. Her biggest jolts of inspiration stem from nature, a variety of film scores, and animals of all kind.

You can connect with me on:

🌐 https://www.hanmgreenbarg.com
🔗 https://www.instagram.com/hanmgreenbargauthor

Also by Han M Greenbarg

Scurts Flightplan

With three months left to live in a stifling, post-nuclear city, Damon Scurto believes he has one last shot at finding the grave of the woman who got away. He is best friends with a guy who eats paper, best frenemies with a convicted killer, and is the bane of his wine-drunk therapist's existence.

Elf Bat Book One Kiah

Twelve years after the ruthless massacre of his parents and most of his kin, eighteen-year-old Elf Bat Kiah lives a life of internalized grief and solitude in his family's cave. The arrival of Fly, a reckless purebred Elf maiden, sparks the flame for revenge and a resurgence of the Bats.

Elf Bat Book Two Sacrifice

The revenge of the Elf Bats has begun in Sidhovvn, each Bat warrior facing down the count who carried out the ruthless slaughter of their family. But in the midst of seeking justice against the purebred king and his soldiers, the sudden emergence of Fly's demon-driven adoptive mother Ixetmori proves to be the bigger test of wills, and the defining moment of what it means to be courageous.

Chehnuh

Year 2018. Chehnuh, a half-elven and sole survivor of his people's genocide, resides quietly in a remote cabin in the Sierra Nevada mountains. No one knows how he came to the United States. No one knows that he is part Elf. He is a mystery to all who meet him until a young widowed mother interrupts his peaceful life with a baby and the shadow of a deadly stalker, forever changing how Chehnuh sees his own past, humanity, and the heroic role he has yet to play in today's world.